An Animalish Man

How often do guys think about sex

G. MLYNEK

Cover design and illustration by Małgorzata Osieleniec
Translated by Agata Dutkiewicz from Polish first edition;
title of original: "Zwierzak: Jak często faceci myślą o
seksie," Copyright © 2017 by Grzegorz Mynarczuk, ISBN:
978-91-983835-1-5
Edited by CreateSpace editing service

CreateSpace revised edition

ISBN-13: 978-9198383539
ISBN: 9198383531

www.gmlynekauthor.com

To my beloved wife
who is always supporting me.

CONTENTS

PRELUDE

Let's not lie to ourselves; men are driven by the evolutionary need to reproduce. The more offspring a man produces, the more of his genes spread around the world; thus, the better accomplishment of the man's evolutionary role on Earth. Of course, the whole process of humankind's survival is more complicated. However, if we were to simplify this issue, would it not be true that it is limited to spreading sperm and taking care of eggs? Isn't the role of a male, after all, to simply have frequent sex? Of course, it would need to be unprotected sex with a fertile female during the fertile part of her cycle—sex that could result in a pregnancy. However, men's sex drive doesn't seem to care about those details.

Let's imagine a real guy; though we should not use the adjective "real," a term so ambiguous that it can have varied interpretations and consequently result in different expectations. Simply imagine a man or a guy—just a typical male. The guy is not a hero of romantic novels, and it never even crossed his mind to think of himself in such categories. His thoughts and skills are more straightforward. A man is prepared for a daily copulation—every day he wakes up with a morning erection. Upon seeing an attractive woman, he always thinks about sex. Men consciously choose women based on their looks, but unconsciously, the choice is based on which woman can be the best birth giver. Our man, if in a relationship with a female, has a natural claim for frequent sexual interactions. If he does not try to get her into bed at every possible occasion, it means that something must absorb his sexual energy—and it cannot be a lover, since every guy has enough strength for a lover and for a partner.

Let's take a look at such a man: the morning has started, and he is slowly waking up. His appearance is not relevant here—he is of an average height and of average weight, just average. Of course, the pattern works the same for everyone, fat or skinny, ugly or pretty; however, let's choose an average man, so we can avoid any additional descriptions of his looks and posture. He is waking up with a morning erection and a smile on his face. A small digression here: the same observation also applies for a female individual, in which case, "a morning erection" would still be appropriate, since the erection of a clitoris appears as often as an erection of a penis, although because of the size of its outer part, it can be unnoticeable. A clitoris is not only the outside "button," but it is also up to six inches of an arborescent, venous organ in the depths of a female body[1]. I apologize for this excursion. Nonetheless, I find it fascinating.

Let's go back to our hero. We will take a look at his actions and thoughts. The latter one is of particular importance for us since we can find out what he truly contemplates in his head—what he would not say out loud, or even admit having had considered. We have a unique chance to find out, for example, how often does he think about sex. Hence, we will continue the story.

"A beautiful day, draw the curtains, but get up, it's cold, so firm, probably in the bathroom, cold, very nice, change tires, why is it dry, uh, too hard, they will not fit, shower, body, nipples, steam…"

This is just typical five seconds of the guy's thoughts, and they are unfortunately incomprehensible. This is precisely how many things are crossing his mind during such a short time—but it is not all of what his mind actually produce. There is much more. Men's thoughts are accompanied by images. If a typical male thinks about female nipples, he imagines their shape and color, as well as the

---

[1] Based on a sonographic three-dimensional image of clitoris, developed by French researchers led by gynecologist Dr. Odile Buisson, urologist, and sexologist Pierre Foldès.

scenery; for example, perky and firm nipples in the soft, bright light of a summer meadow. In order to continue, everything needs to be filtered and converted into a form, which will be comprehensible for the reader. We will begin anew. Maybe we will understand something, and maybe it will be a waste of time...

CHAPTER ONE

"**I** dreamt about something, but I can't remember the details. She was there, and something or someone else was there as well. It doesn't matter—it was cool. Oh, hey! I see you are fully ready. Taking care of you would be a good idea. Your target is taking a shower and doesn't have time today for morning sex. Maybe an opportunity comes in the evening, or maybe I will have quick fun on my own—the never-ending dilemma. Eh, in any case, I can manage in the evening as well."

He sat on the bed and grabbed his penis with his right hand. Slightly squeezing, he started to move the hand, first toward and then away from himself. He didn't need to prepare: he was ready. The penis, as usual in the morning, was fat and firm. From afar he heard that she was finishing her shower. "I need to hurry up." He moved the hand quickly, holding his penis. He lay on his back and bent his head backwards. His hand squeezed and started to go up and down intensely. His face turned red, and the top of his penis began to turn purple. Someone could think that he was too fierce, but the effect was immediate. It was not even a minute when the sperm covered his hand. "Fuck, I don't have any tissues." He needed to use the other hand to take off the whole liquid. He got up and went quickly to the kitchen, carefully washed his hands, and at that point, she came out of the bathroom.

"How did you sleep? What do you want for breakfast?" he asked hastily.

"Hi! Good. You look really tempting, completely naked in the kitchen…Make anything, I need to leave soon."

The first words caused the feeling of temptation rushing through his body, but the end of the sentence diminished any chances for a quickie. Unexpectedly, the memory of the last day before she had moved in came to his mind. He decided that he would have sex only with her. There would be no flirtation with other women. Be-fore he used to have different periods, less active or more active, some even crazy. For example, one summer during the vacation, his only aim was to satisfy himself. If there was an opportunity, he would use it. If there was no prospect, he would spend the whole day with pornography or even go to a gay cinema just so someone would blow him. But now it was sex with only one woman. On that last day, he had a marathon of pornographic videos, just to say good-bye. He thought about that day while making scrambled eggs. "Yes, the best were the ones with group sex." He took out the eggs from the fridge and cracked them open into the bowl. "Truth be told, I never tried any orgy. I would be too scared to catch something. You just walk up to somebody and start. Then someone else joins. You get bored, you change the woman." He scrambled the eggs with a fork, poured oil on the pan, and turned on the cooker. "At that time, I had watched like five movies and masturbated almost non-stop." Next, he chopped the onions. "Break for a beer and food, and then another round." The onions landed on the hot pan. "I forgot the butter." He took the butter out of the fridge and added a spoon. Then he added a bit of sugar. "I don't remember these movies anymore. I only remember some penises and vaginas, a lot of movement and a lot of ejaculations. That was actually what I wanted. After some time, I run out of juice. I think my prostate had to stop working because only a drop of cum would come out, and the balls became smaller. Then I decided to let it go." He added salt and pepper to the bowl and poured everything into the pan. While he was stirring the eggs, he realized that, in fact, the best scenes of sex were the ones with her now, and whenever he masturbated, he would think of her. The eggs were ready. "It's hard again. I need to put on some clothes." He placed the eggs on two plates and went to put trousers on. "Eggs are on the table," he shouted. When he returned, she was sitting at the table eating. He joined, they ate breakfast, and then both went on with their lives.

Ulf left the house and walked toward his car—he would always drive to work. His mother chose his name, but his friends called him Ulfi. His mother had studied a list of names and carefully selected it because she wanted a name that would give her son originality, so he would succeed in life. According to characteristics traditionally associated with this name, a person named "Ulf" should be confident, a good and smart observer, and someone who would enjoy life and its pleasures. Somehow, she missed the fact that such a person also falls easily into conflicts with others, and frankly, Ulf just means "wolf." It's hard to tell whether our Ulf has all of these traits, but his confidence stands out even in the way he walks. His walk is vital and decisive, and when he crosses the street, he has a habit of hopping from a curb onto a road and then jumping on the pavement while getting off a street.

Every day he would drive his car to work. He took family life into account, so he decided to buy a station wagon, but with a sufficiently big engine—just in case. Unfortunately, he regretted it soon after. The car was boring. Despite the large engine, it had an acceleration of a turtle, and it didn't make anyone's head turn. Not surprisingly, it didn't cause any envy among his friends either. Honestly, the car was the subject of many jokes, which described the machine as a "coffin" or a "hearse." Of course, he could not stand it. He decided that since he didn't have kids yet, the car could be upgraded. He invested in wider rims and low-profile tires. At the service station, he lowered and stiffened his car suspension, changed to a sport muffler, and increased the horsepower a bit by installing an additional turbocharger. Of course, the term "a bit" is relative, since in this case, it meant an extra 100 horsepower, which with the unskilled use of a gas pedal could turn the tires into dust within minutes, and with the tires disappearing, so would the monthly salary. Now he felt more comfortable in his "racing car." The V6 engine was playing a symphony, which flattered his ears and triggered admiration among most of his friends. Although the jokes about his vehicle haven't stopped, now they were focused on a superfast coffin but still a coffin. It was not of so much importance for him, though, the adjective "superfast" would enable him to calmly take the jokes. It was also not relevant that the driving quality was closer to a rack wagon—its bottom would feel every single bump on the road. What was important was that he finally felt confident sitting in his car.

Almost every time he would turn on the engine, it

reminded him of all the romantic episodes he had in cars. It was always uncomfortable, but it was also very exciting. He would remind himself of the tiredness, awkward position, painful legs, and bruised elbows, but he would also remember the intensity of fast orgasms. This car had not been tried out yet, and while he was driving, he imagined how he would finally manage to convince her to have sex in it, and how it would be like. He thought they would probably manage to do it doggy style in the back seats, even though there wasn't much space. He had to break rapidly. A red light and a line of cars suddenly appeared in front of him. He stopped just before he hit the bumper of the car stopped ahead of him. His erection disappeared, and thoughts shifted to tasks that were awaiting him at work. They had a new employee. She was an attractive, recently single twenty-something-year-old woman. Today he was supposed to talk to her and discuss a new project for her start at the company. He arrived at work accompanied by thoughts about a project, a new employee, and past car adventures.

While he was walking into his office, he greeted every employee with an honest smile. He always responded to greetings and smirk flirtatiously at women, wondering how many of them find him attractive. The morning passed as he completed his daily responsibilities. It was the most productive part of his day. He tried to focus on work and do all tasks accurately and efficiently. He wanted to do as much as he could so there would be no tasks left for the afternoon because from then on he would get distracted. Since he could not focus anymore, he would spend hours on social interactions. He would pretend he has a work-related task to visit his co-workers' offices and have a chat. He believed that networking is necessary for a successful career, and ultimately, it makes life easier. If someone would ask how his work is doing on a particular task, he would never admit that he accomplished it. He would go back to his room and pretend to work on it, and a moment later he would come out saying that everything is finished. It gave him points for being a good worker while he continued his socializing activities. However, before he could get to that point, he needed to meet this new employee, whose name he still could not remember. They were introduced to each other once, and since then they saw each other only occasionally when they walked by each other in the corridor. Now, they were sitting together in the conference room analyzing papers and planning something. In the past, he would often try to switch the topic to female-male relationships, but today she was the one to start a conversation about how she left her guy. Everyone in the office already knew about it, but of course, everyone pretended not to know when talking with her.

"I am glad to have this job now, after my breakup. I will have more time for myself and for work."

"Did you split with your guy? He pretended to be surprised. "I am sorry about that, but I guess there had to be a reason for that." He smiled.

"Maybe so. I feel that I did the right thing. I am happier, and nowadays I have more energy and time for stuff I have always wanted to do. I have already signed up for yoga."

She straightened her back and put her hands up bending back and stretching after long hours behind a desk. Ulf could not avoid noticing that her breasts pushed the tight shirt so that a bit of her bra was visible around the unbuttoned cleavage. His brain involuntarily started creating images: how does she look in her lingerie? The blood pumped from his heart and flowed through his body toward his penis. He was wondering why he was the first person she has informed about her breakup. It looked like an opportunity; that meant he might have a chance with her. He needed to answer something. "Just not about sex, not about sex!" he thought. He didn't want to switch the conversation to work, so he asked about yoga.

"Yoga? I have never tried."

"It's great. You should also go. It will help you relax."

He thought, "Do I look not relaxed? I would rather say I look horny." He couldn't wait to have sex in the evening, but now he needed a cold shower. He didn't really remember the rest of the conversation. He couldn't even recall her name—they had seen each other barely twice. Right after the meeting, he run to the toilet. He closed the booth doors, released his penis, and speedily rubbed his hand against it until he came. "To the point," as his father used to say. He didn't use his hand to catch the ejaculation, so the liquid splashed on the toilet seat; he had to wipe it out with paper. He took a leak and went back to his office.

During a lunch break, he joined his colleagues at the restaurant on the other side of the street. They were talking about soccer, cars, and vacations, but he was wondering all the time if he should mention the new, attractive employee. More specifically, if he should say that she disclosed her breakup to him first. He already knew what they would say: "She is attracted to you," "She needs a man," and so forth. In the end, he didn't mention it, not because of the possible comments but because of potential competition. It would only encourage them to hit on her more directly. He was the winner for now, and he wanted to keep her for himself.

Since the last conversation, a new employee started to exchange friendly and flirty smiles with him. It started another wave of images in Ulf's mind.

"I have seen it before. Ah yes, at my previous work I also had these smile exchanges, and then eventually, after a week, we met one on one in the social room. We didn't talk—we only examined each other with our eyes. The room had a door which led to a storage for coffee, cups, paper, and other office equipment. I moved toward her, and I delicately stroked her hip. I was amused when I showed her the door. She laughed, but her eyes said no. Still, she didn't walk away. I softly grabbed her hand and led her toward the storage room. She fought slightly, but she followed. I opened the door and slowly pushed her inside. Then I walked behind her. She still resisted a little bit. When I closed us inside, we started to hastily kiss and undress the most necessary parts. I took her from the back. She grabbed my hand and was licking it. I attempted, with the same hand, to cover her mouth so no one could hear her moaning, and I didn't want to scream either. It was one of those double orgasms, which rarely happen to me. I ejaculated and continued until she came, and then I climaxed one more time. After we had finished, we fell on the floor, and of course, at that point, someone came into the social room. We needed to wait about half an hour before it got empty again. We were lucky no one decided to check out the storage room."

Today he had a good day at work. The "social time," as he liked to call his afternoons, was very creative and passed by very quickly. It was already time to leave work. He was going home in a good mood, driving his "family truck." He decided to order some good food at the restaurant or even cook something himself. In his thoughts, he was already having a thrilling evening. Awaiting sex made his mood even better, and his libido was increasing. On the way, he stopped by the supermarket to buy something for dinner. The sexual thoughts appeared again, and it became tight between his legs. He didn't mind the full erection in his trousers as he entered the store. The walk was uncomfortable, and every move would put pressure, and at the same time, stroke against his genitalia. It was so pleasant that he felt the tip of his penis getting moist. Of course, it was not possible to hide the small tent set up between his legs. Usually, he would not pay attention when people looked at his privates, but then he noticed that by the cheese stand there was a long-haired brunette observing him with curiosity. He has poor memory for faces, and this time the image of a woman was pushed into unconsciousness as well, but he remembered her eyes well—green and unnaturally big as if they didn't belong to the rest of the body. He saw that for a split second she looked down and then at him again while putting the gorgonzola back on the shelf. She softly stroked the cheese, with a slow movement her hand went to her body and upward towards her face. She smiled delicately, and Ulf forgot why he was there. He forced himself to take his eyes off the woman and checked the cheese shelf. He stood in front of a row of imported cheese. At that moment, he recalled: spaghetti, parmesan, tomatoes...dinner...sex. "Yes, turn around and walk toward the cashier." Previously, he wouldn't miss out on such a chance. When he got to the cashier, he realized his basket was empty.

While driving a car, he often felt the need to turn into a small street and pleasure himself, but there were too many people, and he could not find a solitary place. The excitement was bothering him—he was disturbed but happy at the same time. He decided to do it while driving on a highway. He would move fast enough so no one could see him and would remain at equal speed with any of the other cars. He turned on the music and entered the highway, and then he saw an unpleasant surprise—a traffic jam. He didn't like a situation that would force him to refrain, but sometimes these situations could not be avoided. The idea of someone seeing him do it in the queue cooled him down, but the next one, that it could be an attractive woman, increased the heat again. Sadly, he had to control himself. "Maybe that's good. I could cause an accident." He heard possible headlines in his head: "The man speeding in a station wagon has caused the biggest collision in the history of our beloved and modernized highway. Unconfirmed sources have revealed to our reporter that the man died while having his hand wrapped around his genitalia. The fingers were so clamped that the medic needed to..."

These were the thoughts that occupied him while he was driving toward his building. He parked the car. As he was exiting the vehicle, he noticed that the lights in his apartment were off, so she probably wasn't home yet. He was hoping she would already be in the apartment. He turned on the light, and a feeling of emptiness struck him. It seemed as some things were missing in the apartment. He was walking toward the fridge to grab a beer when he noticed a note in the kitchen: "I am sorry I cannot tell you personally, but it's better this way. I am leaving you. The rest of my things I will pick up when you're not home, and I will also leave the key..." Ulf stopped reading and looked around the kitchen and then turned his eyes on the letter once again. She mentioned something else that the only thing they had in common was sex, and she wanted something more. He scrunched the note up and threw it into the garbage. He took a beer out of the fridge and headed toward the sofa. The feeling of emptiness was now explained by the absence of her stuff. She took it with her when she left him. He felt utter confusion and didn't know what to think about it. He sat down with a bottle of beer in his hand and turned on the TV, out of a habit and to ease his mood.

The advertisement block was running on his favorite channel. A skinny, clumsy man in glasses is washing a window. An attractive woman in a bathing suit was holding a cup in her hand while giving commands, and then she sat behind the desk and enjoyed her coffee. A guy was playing with his son in a garden, or in a city park, on a sunny day. He smiled while holding up a smiling baby, and in the background, appeared a big logo of an insurance company. A caring father was playing with a child and was putting him into a trolley—the trolley was easy to handle and safe, and even a guy could cope with it. Diapers—a happy female face on the packing, no sign of a man. A middle-aged guy with gray hair, in a suit, was giving advice to a woman on which laundry detergent would be the best for her. Another guy, a businessman, was sitting in front of a laptop and supposedly was completing banking transactions; the background was filled with stock market figures, and behind a glass wall, an endless line of people was passing by while he calmly observed them from behind his desk. A young, beautiful, fragrant man was seen by a woman on the TV screen, and then she turned her head to her ordinary husband sitting on the couch. A half-naked, muscular guy was shaving while a young, attractive woman kissed his smooth cheek.

The advertisements seemed to go on forever, He managed to drink a few beers during that time. He looked at the screen and decided that these ads were immensely stupid. He pointed his index finger at the TV, while simultaneously holding a beer bottle, and he shouted with a slightly intoxicated voice: "Fuck off. I will do what I want!" He was angry and upset and decided to get properly drunk.

CHAPTER TWO

The next day Ulf woke up on the sofa wearing his clothes. There were empty beer bottles all over the table, and an eaten pack of chips on the floor. He had a bad taste in his mouth and was dirty and sweaty—the feeling was irritating. He went quickly to take a shower. He didn't feel like playing around in the shower. He touched his genitalia but resigned at once. He stood with his hands resting on the wall, and he was enjoying the hot water falling down his neck and back. He was alone again. He didn't want to be lonely anymore. He remembered the words from the letter about how sex was the only connecting factor between the two of them and that they had different expectations. He thought they were getting along, but apparently he was mistaken. He felt that he needed to do something. "Change the way I am? Find out what she wants? Maybe I need help. Maybe there is something wrong with me?" Nevertheless, he felt depressed, and he didn't feel like chatting with his buddies or with anyone from the outside. "I will look for something, someone, anything, but first I need to get some fresh air." He was walking through the city when he began to see things in a different light. He did see women, but today they didn't have the usual influence on him. He looked at them almost indifferently. On the one hand, it didn't bother him, but on the other, he started to wonder what happened to his natural desires. Now, when women stopped occupying his mind, he began to notice other people and the details of a city. Others didn't interest him, but he noticed all advertisements spread everywhere across the city. He felt as if he were walking through a bazaar or a fest, and everything looked the same as on TV. There was an attractive couple in their forties with bright smiles. He thought, "It's probably an ad for a travel agency or boner pills." He looked at the billboard with a resigned face. Only after a while, he read the signs. "Do you have issues with hypersexuality? Call us…" He thought, "No sane person would ever want to treat hypersexuality. It's something to cherish." He didn't know why, but he took a photo of an ad with his phone. It was Saturday, and he usually wouldn't leave the house during the weekend—he would rest at home instead.

He needed to relax and calm down. Sex was no longer a way to relax. He hid in his house and reflected. He recalled a conversation with Tess. Now he remembered her name—Tess, from Teresa. She was the one who noticed he looked stressed while they were sitting in the conference room, and then she described how great she felt doing yoga. He didn't feel like exercising among women. Only the gym was an acceptable form of exercise in his opinion, but he decided to give yoga a try. He found the nearest studio and forced himself to leave the house.

"Here I am, at yoga class, and what do I see? A bunch of chicks in tight sportswear, bending and stretching. What sick mind would consider yoga class a good place to stop thinking about sex? Whichever way I turn there are round butts, perky breasts, and tightened backs. OK, there is one guy with dreadlocks and a man-bracelet on his hand. A "bracelet" and a "man"—these two are mutually excluding words. He decided to focus on his workout. It turned out yoga required more effort than he assumed. He tried to complete the exercises correctly, but he failed most of the time anyway. He thought of himself as a fit man. He would regularly go to a gym and ride a bike, but here he couldn't make it. He concluded that he needed to take better care of his body. Halfway through the class he was already exhausted and sweaty. He imagined all the women around him laughing on the inside. At the end, before the final relaxation, he looked around the room and locked eyes with one woman. Honestly, he didn't remember the way she looked. He only noticed that she was young, and her eyes, or rather the expression, told him she wanted him. His eyes had to reflect desire as well—the tight sportswear on a woman aroused him. His penis automatically moved. When they lay down for the corpse pose, he almost fell asleep. He forgot about these eyes, and he was feeling relaxed; his head was filled with pleasant emptiness. However, when he was leaving the class he again felt the glance of the same woman on the corridor. They looked into each other's eyes and the only question in the air was whether they do it at his place or at her place. "My place," she answered. He drove with eyes focused on the red lights of the car in front of him, watching every turn carefully. He felt more peaceful than ever after he left the class, but the meeting with that woman awoke an enormous desire in him. He had never felt such strong temptation. His hands were shaking, and his cock felt stiff and wet on the tip, pressing between his legs. She parked the car, and so did he. He followed her without speaking as if he were on a leash. As soon as they stepped into the apartment, he grabbed her and put her on the first thing that had a suitable height for his hips. They didn't take their clothes off, she only slid her leggings and pants down her thighs, and he took out his penis through his trousers. His penis was ready, hard and firm. She was also prepared, warm and wet, so he went easily inside. He came within a minute, but he didn't worry—he could do it for a long time tonight. He got hard and ready to continue. She was very wet, and he realized that his trousers were getting moist. He felt she would come any moment, and then he began moving his hips faster so that he could ejaculate once more before she climaxed. He grabbed her thighs firmly and pushed rapidly inside her, his hips hitting hard against her cheeks. She was lying on her back with her legs against his chest. Her eyes were closed, and only occasional moans came out of her mouth. He felt her shivering when he ejaculated inside her again. She threw her legs on the other side of the table and slid down, almost falling on the floor. She got up, breathing heavily from exhaustion, and looked at him with a slight smile. They still hadn't exchanged a word. She got up and started undressing while moving to the next room. Ulf took out a bottle of water from his bag, took two big swallows, and looked at her. She was standing there naked at the edge of a dimmed room, and her hand reached out for the bottle, so he threw it in her direction. She caught it easily with her right hand and took few big sips. She did it so carelessly that the water spilt out of her mouth and went down her cheeks and further along her body. The small strain of water was traveling through her neck onto her right breast and stopped on the hard, pointy nipple before it dropped down on the floor. The generous stream flowed down her neck, chest, and further down her belly until they ended at her pubic hair. When the hair couldn't absorb the water anymore, the drops went down on the inner side of her thighs. This view aroused him again. She threw the empty bottle on the floor, turned around, and went inside the room. Her figure was getting smaller until the moment she disappeared completely in the dark. He headed toward her, taking his clothes off. When he entered the room, she turned on a lamp on the bedside table. It lit only the corner of the place. It turned out to be a bedroom. She sat on the edge of the bed. He came up to her, and she grabbed his ass and pushed him toward herself. He felt the softness of her lips and the warmth of her tongue on his penis. After some time, he pushed her on the bed and lay on the side next to her, with his legs toward her face. He lifted her right leg and looked for her clitoris with his tongue. Sometimes, he would push his tongue inside her vagina and go back to the clitoris or put his finger inside and look for the bump at the entrance of her vagina. She would bend as if she wanted to run away. She was salty from all the sweat and sperm and slightly sour from her liquid. She was sucking on his penis, wet from the cum and her own fluid. They went over every imaginable position calmly, without a hurry this time. At some point, she lay on her left side, and he knelt behind her. He entered her slowly, forcefully holding her hips, and he massaged her anus with his left thumb. The sight of his penis disappearing inside her continuously was turning him on. She turned on her back uncovering her breasts. He grabbed her left boob and squeezed it hard. She screamed out of pain but also out of pleasure. She didn't take off his hand. He continued while she screamed louder and louder. Then she turned rapidly on her left side again while her open right hand slapped his cheek. He was shocked and angered. First, he thought it could have been an accident. Then he looked at her and saw a grin on her face. She did it on purpose! He was furious. He turned her on her belly and pushed his penis inside her while pressing his body against hers. He slipped his hand under her arm and reached for the back of her head to grab her hair. The other hand he used to clutch her wrist, he immobilized her lying down on her. He was fucking her as hard as he could. She screamed with satisfaction. After a while, he calmed down. He moved his left hand under her belly and started to play with her clitoris. It was not comfortable, but he was still aggressively pushing his penis inside her. He breathed deeply and sweat intensely. She moaned even louder now, almost screaming. He felt her climax was coming. He slowed down, intentionally prolonging the feeling. He was also ready, and after they had come, they lay next to each other, sweaty and exhausted. Surprisingly, he was still hard and ready to continue. She also noticed that and placed her head on her elbow. She got up and sat on his phallus, face to face. She started to ride him, and he thought he could no longer continue, but his penis ejaculated inside her again. She fell on him and a moment later slid on the side. She covered herself with a blanket and silently prepared to sleep. Ulf was also sleepy, but he didn't stay. He got up and put on his clothes. He decided not to wake her up. He went to the kitchen, drank a glass of water, and left.

When he got to his bed, he thought that this was the best sex of his life, but he also felt that he didn't want to go to her or know who she is. If he met her on the street, then yes, but he would not look for her. As he was falling asleep, he recalled the scenes from this fruitful night. The excitement reappeared. He grabbed his penis and satisfied himself.

When he woke up the next morning, he realized that he was back to his old self. Suddenly, women reappeared in his mind. He was still upset about the breakup, but he felt mostly desire. He was surprised how quickly he returned to his old habits. He knew that, from now on, he will be his old self—an animal. Only in the depths of his soul he felt unresolved issues. "Can I continue to live like this, and do I really want to? I don't want to think about this. I will put it off for later, and I will not feel bad about it. I will not plan, think, or choose. Why no one will tell me there is nothing wrong with this, that it's OK, that I can? I can!" He shouted the last phrase, but it didn't convince him.

Suddenly the phone rang. More precisely, it was the sound of an alarm on his phone. At first, when he looked at the screen, he didn't understand. "Make an appointment: hypersexuality." "Ah yes, a moment of weakness. I need to delete this picture." He started to look for the file in his phone's gallery. As he clicked on the image, he accidentally turned on an app, which marked a text from a photo, specifically the phone number. The ad-dress book switched on suggesting to save a number. That is when he noticed that the number had already been saved in his phone as "hypersexuality." He found it weird since he couldn't remember saving this number. He wanted to delete it, but of course, he clicked instead on dialing. He hated when a smartphone, a computer, or any other electronic device wouldn't listen to him, and instead, it would make its own choice. He wanted to crash his phone against the wall. Meanwhile, the sound of a female voice resonated from the speaker. The voice was happy and smooth. It woke up his imagination. He couldn't resist talking to a beautiful, sensual, probably young woman—even if it was only for a minute. She was probably sitting in a miniskirt, with her legs crossed and her thighs exposed and was wearing glasses—intelligent and flirtatious. She proposed a meeting in an office. As a joke, he said he can meet at 6:00 a.m., with a disappointed voice. "Of course, no problem," she answered. "We are available twenty-four-seven for our clients. I'm really excited about our meeting." He was surprised and distracted. As always, he got tangled into some meeting just because of some attractive woman. He had to change that early-hour meeting at least. "I just noticed I can't meet so early, but eight o'clock in the morning would work for me. I will manage to come be-fore my work," he said. "As you wish. I will send you a note with the address and instructions by text. Thank you for calling. I hope to see you soon." He answered, "Thank you." He paused for a moment and realized that now he had an appointment he didn't want to have.

CHAPTER THREE

Did you wonder how often do you think about sex? Were you curious if other guys think about sex as often as you do? The man who asked Ulf these questions was sitting behind the desk in front of a bright window. It was hard to examine his face. Ulf had to squint his eyes, and it made him tired and irritated. He only noticed that the man was rather short, with a small belly, gray-haired, and in a polo shirt, as if he has just come back from a golf court. An attractive, long-haired blonde was sitting by the side of his desk wearing typical office clothing. He couldn't see the color of her outfit, but he could notice how tightly the skirt rested on her thighs. The sight of her skirt and how soft her thighs looked made him stare. On her right leg, crossed over her knee, she held a notebook or some other device. Now and then she would mark something.

"What do you think, how many times did you check out my assistant since you entered my office?

Before you sat down, who did you notice first?"

He tried to answer this question, but he couldn't. He just didn't know.

"You looked twenty-three times at her within five minutes," said the man, while watching the computer screen on his desk. "So more or less it makes every thirteen seconds." He glanced at Ulf expressively.

An assistant, whose name he didn't remember despite their introduction, smiled friendly without any embarrassment. He concluded that she was not as attractive as he thought, but her revealed thighs were quite arousing. His brain automatically created images of her naked in a bed, covered partly by bedsheets, in a morning sun shining through the window.

"You know, we have cameras here," he continued. "Your stares were focused on my eyes or somewhere near my head. The glimpses toward my assistant included her whole body, especially her thighs, but no shoes. Don't worry, that's normal, or at least within the norm. There were some here who had a hundred glimpses with-in five minutes, so they looked at her every three seconds. Can you imagine?"

Ulf had shaken off the image of a naked assistant and straightened his back rapidly.

"OK, Mr. Smith." That's how his conversation partner introduced himself. "But why do you do all this?" he asked while at the same time he thought that his last name was like a cliché from a bad criminal movie.

"Since you here, Mr...." Mr. Smith made a pause and looked at him. "Excuse me, would you mind reminding me your name?"

"Ulf, just Ulf."

"A name worth writing down."

"It just means 'wolf.'"

"OK, I see. As I was saying, since you're here, that means you had been wondering about your desires, your sexual appetite. Is that correct?"

Ulf nodded inconclusively with his head.

"So, we have an interesting proposition for you, and the best part is that you will not need to change your lifestyle. We even don't want you to change it. That is what the study is about. We, so to speak, check the sexual appetite of people and test an innovative supplement, mostly vitamins. We want to understand the human behavior during their experience of sexual drive. The offer is simple. We will set an appointment for you with a previously selected woman, you do your part, and we gather the results of our study."

"Interesting and surprising offer. It sounds a little bit like an escort agency, only I am on the escort side."

"There is no need to worry. The women also join this study so you will meet with other participants of the experiment. I have to make it clear: a lot of people experienced positive changes in themselves throughout the study. Usually, these are the individuals who are addicted to sex or, at least, very sexually active. The experiment helped them to understand and control their needs. We will make it easier for you to have an insight into your desires, to use and master them. Thanks to us, you will also notice other things, and you will stop to consider your drive as an issue—it will become an asset. Anyway, you can have a look yourself."

Mr. Smith handed Ulf a file with photos of the participants: men and women recommending the experiment. He noticed that none of the women in the archive would hear no from him.

"Will I also be in such a file?"

"Only if you will agree. And I think you will, because—believe me—you will be satisfied, and you will recommend our study to others with confidence."

He was browsing through the pictures when he heard an answer to a question which appeared in his mind.

"Yes, you will be able to meet all these women. You know what? Please, choose one for the first trial appointment. Even tomorrow. What do you think?"

Ulf thought, "Ulf, brother, all this seems very suspicious. This whole environment, the Smith surname, the attractive woman who diverts your attention. Also, there is nothing for free in this world. Of course, they are hiding something, but...I don't feel like analyzing this. I don't care! I will meet a few and resign. I cannot deny some women satisfaction, especially in the name of science." He smiled involuntarily. "Only for a couple of days."

Before he left, the blonde took him to the treatment room. There, a woman wearing a nurse's attire showed him a chair to sit on. Her appearance was the opposite of the blonde. It was an ordinary room with an ordinary woman: a slim, short brunette with dark eyes—typical Spanish beauty. At first, you probably would not pay attention to her if she was the one next to Mr. Smith's desk; however, after the close examination, she would be the one to choose. Before he realized, she had already collected his blood for testing and given him the vitamins shot. He looked at the label on the bottle and noticed partly the sign "vitaminum." Next, everyone said their friendly good-byes with him, and he left the building. He felt like taking a walk, he didn't want to get into a car yet. He was strolling down the pavement and was in an astonishingly good mood. He was euphoric and convinced that this decision was right, that a new period of his life had just started. This idea made him walk down the street with a satisfied, idiotic smile.

The only thing that changed in his life was the way he was getting to meet women, or in other words, he didn't have to get the women anymore. He would pick up the phone and receive instructions. Usually, these included a hotel and a room number. He would meet one woman for a few times. Then, after about a week, the female participant changed. They never met in the same hotel room. It was so convenient! He saved a lot of energy, and he also avoided unnecessary frustration. And moreover, he could also practice his skills.

Yes, he had amazing skills. As Superman had his powers, so did Ulf. He could recognize when the climax of a woman is near, when it comes, and whether it's real. If the orgasm was real, he was trying to prolong it and wait as much as he could before ejaculating. They would climax together, and he would even feel like meeting her again. When he felt that a woman was faking, he didn't wait for nothing. Only his pleasure was relevant, as well as the relief he felt after his own orgasm. Sometimes, a woman who pretended would change her mind during penetration, and her moans were no longer faked, but Ulf didn't care at that point. He finished quickly and left the woman unsatisfied. This was his little revenge for her being fake. He was able to perfect and practice his skill without any negative feelings, since the women the organization sent didn't care about him. This was only an experiment. It allowed him to practice his ability almost to perfection. He was happy about this benefit of this study. Unfortunately, he couldn't fully use his talent because it seemed that the women he was meeting didn't focus so much on pleasure. He felt like a subject of an experiment, but he didn't care, and he would quickly forget these worries. He felt good. No hunting—only phone calls with an address. Ulf was finally satisfied—he felt relieved when women left in a good mood. "Exactly, it was always this way. I was used and manipulated. I danced as they played, just because I wanted to sleep with them. Oh, it's so good not to worry about it anymore, that if I do something wrong, there would be no sex for a week as a punishment."

His day passed by on fucking, eating, and working. He was the perfect subject for this study—he regularly attended assigned injections, and whenever called in, he would be there with no buts. That would probably last for months, or even years, if not for those damn phone calls.

The "damn phone calls" were those made by a certain lady. He had to pick his phone up because that was the only way to find out about the arranged meetings. Both numbers were private, so he would never know which one was calling. It was always the same—a female voice asked him a series of questions and then hung up: "Did you notice how they look at you? Do they desire you? Are you sure?"

He didn't notice it at first; why would he? He is a guy, and he doesn't have the time or a need to guess what others think. He met with them for one aim and didn't examine them carefully—especially he didn't notice the way they looked at him. Now, when he thought about it, he realized they did look at him with desire, but their behavior told him something more— they wanted him, but they didn't prolong the intercourse. These females were more impatient. It was visible in their eyes and orgasms that they didn't care about his experience. They loved when he finished inside them and were happy and satisfied, but they would not talk with him and left quickly.

The phone calls continued—always the same female voice and the same questions, which, at some point, Ulf started answering in his head. "Did any of them ever give you a blowjob?" Negative answer. There was no oral sex. Truth be told, they were mostly wet and ready as soon as he entered the room.

"What do you think, how long can you keep it up?" An elusive answer. "I can always manage! OK, lately I need a bit more time, but it might be only my imagination."

"Do you think you give them anything? Or maybe they take something from you?" No specific answer, but he thought, "What are you talking about, woman? I give them nothing and they take nothing. It is just great!"

"And have you noticed any changes in yourself?" A negative answer.

No, he didn't notice anything. He decided to stop picking up the calls. These questions started to scare him, and he was fed up with this female voice—she made him feel stupid.

It seemed as if those "damn calls" happened daily. He picked the phone up despite his resolution, hoping that this one would give him a hotel room rather than a series of questions. He knew that he would have to confront the female voice at some point. He heard the phone ringing again and the familiar female voice. This time he didn't hang up the phone.

"Do you have fun?" the voice in the speaker asked.

"Why? Do you want to have fun as well? You can come for a visit. I'm sure you know my address since you already have so much information about me." He heard a laugh.

"Me? No. I don't want what these women want. You are avoiding me lately."

"If hanging up the phone means I'm avoiding you, then yes, I do."

"Don't be stupid. You are avoiding me. You don't notice me on the street."

There was a teasing atmosphere, a form of flirt. He had to admit that he liked the tone of her voice and probably would even regret if she stopped calling him.

"But I don't know you," he answered.

"Oh god, how can you be so stupid? I'm losing my patience. Are you sure you don't know me? Look around, for god's sake. Why do you think they need your sperm? Use your fucking brain! Didn't you notice someone is missing in the office? Call me back when you start thinking!" She hung up.

The sudden change of her tone shocked him. The voice was filled with anger and impatience but remained friendly. This made him think. He heard that voice be-fore. "What was that about the sperm? Why would anyone need it? Maybe I really should reflect on it," he thought. "Have you noticed any change in yourself?" The question was resonating in his head. "No, I didn't. They stopped calling as well! I walk around with my dick like a baseball bat—I have enough of this!"

He finally understood. He grabbed his mobile and dialed her number. He knew who she was. It's always darkest before the dawn. It's like looking for scissors in a cupboard: you see them but do not notice. It was Tess. Of course he had her number—he had contact info of every female in the office.

"Hi! What is it all about?"

"We shouldn't speak on the phone, let's meet," Tess answered.

CHAPTER FOUR

They decided to meet in a public space, a nearby restaurant where everyone from the office gathered for lunch. They didn't want to raise any suspicions, but they worked together, so meeting after work in a commonly attended place was not unusual. As soon as Ulf saw Tess, he started noticing how every time he had seen her, she was pushing her breasts forward and exposing a piece of lacy underwear. This image was reappearing in his mind every time he saw her. Now she looked serious, and her eyes were worried. He waved at her and asked with a gesture if she wanted anything to drink. She nodded, so he came up to the bar and ordered two beers. He thought, "She looks worried. It's sad to see such a beautiful woman upset, but I will find something to cheer her up." He had already forgotten the aim of this meeting. He walked toward her with a flirtatious smile and asked, "What's up? How are you?"

"You are not here to hit on me, are you? Sit, this is serious." She cooled him down quickly.

He suddenly noticed that it was not a worry in her eyes. It was nervousness, even fear. He put down the bottles and sat down on the opposite side of the table. Then suddenly he remembered why he came here.

"OK, what is this all about?"

"Frankly, I'm not sure myself, but I know you are in danger. Do you remember Frank from the office? The one with abundant hair?"

"Yes. What about him?"

"What do you mean 'What about him?'? Haven't you noticed? He disappeared!"

"So what? Maybe he didn't like the job."

"You don't understand. He disappeared without a trace. He is not in the office, and you cannot contact him in any way. And I left him the digits for Haxegen as well."

"What Hexagen? And what do you mean that you left the digits?"

"How can you be so ignorant! Hexagen is the scientific institute"—she made quotation marks with her fingers—"that sends you the women."

"Ah! I didn't notice that this was their name. Well, but what is your connection with all this?"

"It's my side job. I recruit the guys for them but not directly. Do you remember how you already had their number in your phone? I put it there. I have to find healthy, sexually active men. I slip the fliers and the phone contact of Hexagen in such a way that guys make a decision to go to the meeting themselves. When guys go there, most of the time they agree to cooperate," Tess explained hurriedly.

Ulf couldn't pretend that being a subject of manipulation didn't surprise him. Still, he didn't understand why he would be in danger.

"OK, if you don't want me to go, I will not. I was planning to end it anyway," he lied.

"It's not that simple. You don't get it!" She noticed she had been speaking too loudly. She looked around to see if anyone was watching them. "I think you are in danger," she continued with a more relaxed tone. "Do you remember Frank?"

"Yes, yes, you already said, the one with abundant hair, the one who disappeared."

"Exactly. I think he also wanted to resign and stopped coming to get injections. I was watching him. He was changing. He started to look bad, like a guy with cancer." Her hand slightly twitched.

"Tess, calm down." He called her by her name for the first time. "I'm sure he's fine." He wanted to stroke her hand, but she moved it back. "Maybe he got sick, and he is undergoing a treatment somewhere?"

"Ulf"—she now looked straight into his eyes with a composed and convincing look—"people are missing. There is some deadly drug in the injection, and you are the next one to disappear. Don't you understand? When was your last injection?"

"No and no. I don't remember when was my last injection. Some time ago. Whatever. What people are missing? Is there anything else?"

"No"—she said hesitatingly—"but it remains suspicious. And you need to get a new dose of these meds, just in case. I need to find out more." She got up and grabbed her coat.

"So first you are calling me all this time, then you have nothing for me, and now you want to run?"

"I didn't want to meet you. The phone calls were supposed to make you think, but the case of Frank changed the situation. I wanted to warn you."

"I feel warned. Now that I'm here, you need to explain to me what do you know and what do you guess. For example, why do they want my juices? You were bothering me about that on the phone almost every day."

She stopped, looked at him confused, and asked, "What juices? Ah, do you mean your sperm?" She sat down at the table again. "You will not believe me anyway."

"Try."

"In a huge oversimplification, they genetically modify your sperm so that these women can bear a baby of another man. I see the way you look at me. You don't believe me. Whatever."

"That's not it. It's not like I don't believe"—his voice was unconvincing—"it just seems technically impossible."

"Ah, yes? Are you a professor of genetics? You better go and get me something to drink."

He got up from the table and wondered what to order on the way to the bar. He didn't feel like having a beer but he ordered it anyway. A TV at the bar showed a picture of some victim, a guy with abundant hair. "Ah, the world is filled with so much violence, and the media are also driving it." He paid for drinks, and as he was coming back, he noticed a fearful expression on the girl's face.

"What happened?" he asked and sat down.

"What, you didn't see? Frank is dead." She pointed at the TV.

He examined the screen more carefully, and sure, it was a picture of Frank. He listened while the reporter explained that they were looking for people who knew this man in order to identify him. He felt uneasy. None of his colleges or family had died yet. He drunk from one of the glasses he held in his hands. The worst part of it all was that this whole story suddenly became more valid. He sat down with both glasses and moved one toward Tess. She drank half of it at once. She waited a few seconds before finishing the rest with one gulp.

"I think I need some air." She got up and moved

toward the exit.

He also got up and tried to finish his beer. He thought the second one was not necessary, especially since he drove there. He left the beer unfinished and followed Tess outside. She was walking toward his vehicle. She turned around and told him that it would be best if they drive somewhere. It didn't matter where, just away.

He drove toward the highway, so they could go straight ahead with no interruption and with no particular aim.

"Maybe we should go to the police," he suggested, breaking the silence.

"Speak for yourself. You know, Ulf, I just thought, I'm not the one in danger. I'm just guessing, I don't know what are they doing and why, so I'm not going to expose them. They also need me for the recruitment. A job like any other.

"So, are you planning to continue?" he asked with disbelief.

"No, maybe not, but I don't want to raise any suspicion. I will just find a way to end it, and I will not involve myself with all this anymore. I am definitely not going to the police."

He nodded. The thoughts were gathering in his head. "Where should I drive? I don't know, straight ahead, I will come up with something later. The smartest option would be to withdraw and do nothing, back off, let them experiment, let them do what they want, but without me. But what if the poisoned injection is real? There is nothing wrong with me after all, I'm healthy, right? Did I get sick lately?" Then he recalled the feeling of hangover he had in the morning despite not drinking anything the previous night and that after every injection he felt especially good. "I need to do something. I need to act be-cause maybe I'm really at risk of dying. At least I need to solve the drug issue."

"OK, what else do you know? Also, how do you know all of this? The genetic modification of sperm and Frank's death. You seemed to be fairly convinced about it. And about the drug in the injections?"

"What are you suggesting? That I'm involved in this?"

"I'm not sure, but you seem to know a hell lot about it."

"I only connected the dots, Ulf. Our office friend would regularly receive these injections, but at some point, he stopped going. I watched him. He started to lose his health. Of course, he may have been sick, but then he disappeared with no trace. The TV broadcast only confirmed my worries. If he had died "normally," it wouldn't be mentioned all over the news." As she was saying "normally," she made a gesture of quotation marks in the air. "Doesn't it seem suspicious to you? I'm convinced there is some deadly drug in the injections."

She looked back at the city from afar.

"And the sperm," she continued. "I found out accidently when I overheard a conversation. One of the lab ladies said in the smoking room that they have a lot of women willing to be impregnated and they 'cannot keep up with delivering all these mutants.' I guessed that they make some mutation or modification on guys. I'm not sure myself, but you give them your genetic material, and they use it to impregnate women. This is not an official experiment, think about it."

"Do you smoke?"

"What?"

"Do you smoke? Eh, never mind. But why do they do all this? If they want women to bear someone else's children, they can use in vitro. No? Anyway, why would women want to participate in that? And guys as well. It's enough to pay them for sex."

"Why pay if they do it for free?" She looked at him with concern. "I didn't figure out yet why they do it. And as for women…this I can understand. That's our nature. It's like with orgasms. You men want it quickly and often; we prefer the quality. You have millions of little guys; we have only one egg. You throw the seeds on the desert into a pot; we take care of those pots. So when we catch a seed, it's going to be the best one. In conclusion, if I want to have a child, I also want to choose the best father."

"Well, for that you have a sperm bank."

"Oh well, with all the losers who are so low on money that they have to sell their sperm!"

They continued to drive silently. Ulf started to make an action plan. First, he needed to convince Tess to come to his place—he still had some questions to ask.

"I'm tired. I need to rest first. If you want, you can stay at my place and sleep there."

He pretended to be indifferent, so she didn't think he was trying to get her into his bed. Of course, he desired to do that despite the whole situation. He turned around and drove back to the city. After a long silence, Tess answered that she can stay at his place because she didn't want to sleep alone. His heart twitched as he felt an opportunity. He couldn't believe himself, even his penis grew at the mere thought of having sex with her. She had to find her exceptionally attractive. "But what about the billboard?" Unexpectedly, his thoughts turned toward the advertisement.

"But what about the billboard? Why do they advertise themselves? They try to stay hidden, no?" he asked.

"Ah, you mean that billboard? Actually, that was a fascinating marketing experiment." Tess got slightly more excited. "You know, I studied marketing. They explained it to us during training, when I started the job. There is only one billboard in downtown, and it has a subliminal message. Typically, it is taken for a travel agency ad. Only if certain circumstances are met, for example a mood, a person can perceive this ad as interesting."

He couldn't really take it seriously, but it didn't surprise him either. He saw a whiskey ad: a glass of alcohol on ice, where an image of a skull was hidden inside an ice cube. He didn't remember what that was supposed to mean. Either that it kills, or it's dangerous, and all the tough guys drink it? They were getting closer to his house. He parked his car on the street, as usual. In the apartment, he asked her if she would like anything to drink. She asked for something strong and communicated that soon she would be off to sleep. He still hoped he could have sex with her. They sat at the kitchen table with only a dimmed light. They were sipping on a golden liquor from glasses.

"So, when did you have your last injection?" she asked.

"I'm not sure, but I think it was about two weeks ago."

"Not good, that's the same scenario as in the case of Frank. They probably took you off meds. Maybe you couldn't do the job anymore."

"What? I couldn't do the job? You must be joking!"

She laughed. "I knew I would hurt your ego." She

got serious again. "You need to go there and get the injection. It will keep you alive at least. Do you understand?"

"Yes. I guess so. If all of this is true. But what next? If they want to cut me off...I have a better idea"—he got excited suddenly—"but I will need your help!"

"I don't want to have anything to do with it anymore."

"I know, but you said yourself that you don't want to raise any suspicions, so you can't just leave. I want you to go there, show up, and communicate that you are go-ing on vacation or something like that."

"OK then, but how would that help you?"

"Make it easier for me to enter the building. I will hide in your car so you can let me in. The rest I can handle myself."

"You are talking nonsense! Better idea? Definitely stupider. They surely monitor everything. Anyway, why do you want to get inside?"

He just knew what needed to be done. It seemed simple and obvious to him. "So, if this serum is so important to them, I will just steal it. It' genius. I will bargain for my life! I will steal the serum probably from the lab!" he said with excitement.

"Do you mean the injection, the drug, yes? You're crazy!"

"There must be someone who can help me, there must...Seriously, they cannot be that secured, safe...I will steal it, and then I will see," he talked incoherently.

"Ulf, it's nonsense! Even if I would get you into the building, I don't have access to the lab. And even if you succeed in that, then what?"

("What am I saying? I'm no fucking Bond, but I have to do, for fuck's sake, anything. Why do I swear so much in my head? I'm going to die anyway, so who cares?")

"I don't know. I will inject one as soon as I can, just in case, and then I will steal as many as I manage to carry. This will give me time. I don't know exactly what I'm going to do, what I'm going to do next, but it's a good plan. Since I will die anyway, what do I care, right? I need to plan everything. I need to get some sleep. What time do you go there?"

"In the morning, before work," she answered with resignation. "I go there only for a second, take my fliers, and leave."

"That's perfect! We will drive my car to your place and change to yours to drive us there. I will hide, get off at the underground parking, and enter the building. You will take care of your business, and I will handle it from then on."

She looked at him with disbelief. "I don't think you understand what you're getting into. They have cameras, security. They will surely notice you."

Ulf didn't pay attention to her words. He felt he was

in a trance—he was unusually animated, and he even forgot that he wanted to bang Tess. She, on the other hand, noticed that he was unreasonable. She knew that his plan didn't make sense, but she was unable to stop him. She finished her drink and decided that she would help him anyway. She would drive there as if nothing happened and take the fliers. He would try to sneak into the building, and she would just get back to her car and leave.

They were talking for a while—or rather, she was answering questions that Ulf had in mind. Most of them were left unanswered, but she was tired and unable to think. Whereas he was walking around the kitchen, and when he thought he had learned everything, he said good night and went to sleep at the living-room sofa without even looking back at her.

CHAPTER FIVE

Tess entered the elevator and drove upstairs to the office. She was supposed to see it for the last time. Tess was thinking how not to reveal her real intentions. She would do what she always did. As if nothing unusual was happening, she would take some fliers, exchange a few words with someone, and inform that she needed to leave to get to her work. As she was making this plan in her mind, she almost believed it herself, and she thought it could actually work and help him. She tried not to get distracted by the thought of him sneaking between the cars on the underground parking lot, so he could enter the emergency staircase unnoticed. "I'm only getting fliers," she thought, trying to convince herself. It was an early morning, and there were only a few people in the office sipping their coffee and yawning. She passed by a receptionist, who greeted her as usual, but they didn't exchange a single word. As she entered a small room filled with desks, she said hi to the people she would usually see but didn't stop to talk to anyone. She explained that today she needed to work early, so she would only pick up some fliers. From the cupboard at the wall, she took out a pile of cards. She left, walked by the receptionist again, and said good-bye, waving with her hand filled with cards. She stopped for a second and told the receptionist she would leave for a short vacation. "Now you're on your own, Ulf," she thought. She entered the elevator, and then she got into the car and drove away. Her cooperation with Hexagen had ended.

Meanwhile, Ulf was climbing the stairs as he assumed everyone would choose the elevator. He stopped at the Hexagen floor and slightly opened the exit door to observe if anyone was crossing the corridor. According to Tess, this was the floor where he could find the lab. Through a gap, he noticed there was only one entrance with a security code next to it and a camera above. He guessed that would be the right door. He didn't know if someone was monitoring the camera, or it was only recording the image, but the bigger problem was the code, which he didn't know. He decided to wait until someone came and started to enter the code. He had come up with a plan yesterday evening when Tessy—he liked to call her that—already had dozed in his bed, and he was lying on the sofa unable to sleep. He had tried to talk to her. Her face didn't have the same worried looked as before. Everyone looks peaceful and beautiful when sleeping. Later, he had sat down at his computer and drudged hours, looking for some information about Hexagen but found nothing, not even a website. He had to do some-thing, at least inform someone about all this. It seemed impossible that no one knew about their business. He had understood that if he had skills to genetically modify sperm, he would also hide it. "If something is not on the Internet, it doesn't exist," he had thought. The reason why he didn't find any information about them could be much simpler: Hexagen regularly deletes any information about them. He needed to push some buttons to retrieve some information, so he put desired words online, and those interested could find it. He had found some random online forums that focused on sex, genetic modification, and secret institutions, so he typed in: "I have Hexagen genetic modification serum and I'm look-ing for an antidote." He was desperate.

His thoughts were interrupted by the sound of steps on the corridor. He waited for a few seconds and slightly opened the door. He had binoculars ready in his hand so he could overlook when someone puts in the code. This idea seemed brilliant at 2:00 a.m. in the morning. He assumed that digital camera zoom may not do the trick, and the quality wouldn't be good enough to see the hand of someone from afar. His telescopic lens would not be handy in such circumstances, so he found old theatrical binoculars, which laid hidden in his drawer for ages, probably not used even once. It was a family souvenir with which he played as a child. Some man walked through the corridor but passed by the lab door, at least so he thought. "Just remember, you cannot stay behind that door for too long. Once I stood there, out of curiosity, and as soon as I tried to open the door, someone appeared immediately. I had to show my ID and prove that I work for them. You need to quickly put in the code and enter as if you do it every day," he recalled her words. The next person, a short woman, walking through the corridor stopped next to the door that interested him. He was watching her fingers typing in the code, and he realized that the idea of the binoculars was ridiculous: he couldn't see anything through the tiny lenses, especially due to his hands shaking from excitement. In general, the whole plan— as genius as it seemed during the night—turned out to be unrealistic, and the idea of overseeing the code this way was naive at best. Unfortunately, he didn't have a choice anymore—he had to try again. When the next person appeared in front of the door, he had his phone ready, and he was recording a video. Surprisingly, the quality turned out to be good enough to clearly see the movement of fingers. Then he came up to the door and typed in the correct combination of numbers. The doors opened, and he found himself in an unknown territory. He wanted to find a quiet place, so he could look around, check where the cameras are, and decide which direction to go. However, the doors led straight into the lab, where some people in white coats were working. All of them turned toward him as he entered. There was no way he could look around. He greeted everyone hurriedly and pointed at the door suggesting that he had forgotten something. He wanted to get out of their sight as soon as possible. One person answered back, and the rest seemed to be uninterested in his presence. He walked toward the opposite doors, which were also secured by a code. He typed in the previous one, and surprisingly, the door opened. He found himself in a treatment room, where he would usually get his injections. The room next to the Smith's office, but at least nobody was here, and he had some time to make a decision about how and where to start his search of what he needed—the serum. "I'm almost confident that I saw this Latina in the lab. Very attractive. I would do her if I had a chance." He smiled. "Jesus! Fo-cus, bro! That's not what you came here for. The vial! Yes, there was a cabinet with some vials in the lab, but I can't just go back there and steal it in front of them." He walked around the room like a lion in the cage. "I'm lucky anyway that nobody is here." He looked around nervously. He didn't spot any cameras, but he noticed a closed bucket for used needles and syringes. He knelt, opened the bucket, and threw the content on the floor. He unreasonably browsed through a pile with his hand, but that's when he saw it. There it was—an open but half-full flask with a familiar "vitaminum" sign. He couldn't believe it. "I guess I have more luck than wisdom." He was still down on his knees and looked at the nearby desk where he saw a tape and a plastic container. He grabbed them and used the tape to close the flask and put it in the container. He found what he wanted, but he needed more of that. When he got up, he caught himself forgetting to plan how to leave the building unnoticed. Somehow it escaped his mind last night. "First, I need to try to find more of these vials. Later I will come up with an exit plan." It seemed natural to him that he should go back the same way he entered— through the lab. "Maybe I will see some more of this drug on the way." He typed in the code again and put his head through the door. Then he immediately saw the Latina pointing at the door he was about to open. She was talking to two security guards. He closed the door before they could notice him. He needed to escape. He didn't have a choice—he had to go through Smith's office and hope that nobody would be inside. He opened the door—they weren't secured—and found the room empty. He moved farther toward the assistant's office. Luckily, she wasn't there either. It seemed that he was a bit disappointed he could not see her sexy thighs again. He knew he was close the exit.

He had to push forward but noticed something interesting on the desk. Two shelves with incoming and outgoing mail. He opened the shelves without any reflection and took out an envelope, wrote down an address, put the serum inside, and placed the envelope onto the outgoing drawer. At this point, the door handle to Smith's office twitched. He dashed in the opposite direction, opened the next door, and suddenly he felt a blow. He lost consciousness.

He woke up on a leather sofa with a headache. He slowly opened his eyes, and the light coming through the window blinded him. He saw the shape of Smith, who was talking to a security guard. He heard bits of the conversation. "Did you search him?" The guard nodded. "He didn't have anything on him, also no wiretap…" Ulf slowly raised his body and sat. Then he glanced at Smith, who noticed his movement and smiled mockingly at him. He could only see this annoying smile at the center of a bright room. He had to squint his eyes, and he couldn't see clearly, which also angered him. "What a ridiculous laugh, a miserable clown. How can such a person get into a high position and power? Hypocrisy and slyness, it's obvious! Damn, I have known it from the beginning. Why didn't I say no then?" The guard moved closer to him and stood by his side. Ulf noticed his enormous back and hand of the size of a bread loaf. Smith started talking from behind his desk.

"I think you have already met my personal security guard." He laughed sarcastically. "What did you imagine, Ulf? That you will come in and steal our serum just like that? Our wolf got a bit too wild. And what would you do with it anyway? Go to the police? You must be stupid."

Ulf tried to get up, but a headache made it impossible. He grabbed his neck and hissed with pain. He felt as if he had a hangover.

"In principle, I wanted to throw you out on the street straight away, but you fascinated me. No one was brave enough, or stupid enough, to attempt such a thing. Besides, I also had to make sure you won't take anything from here. Does your head hurt? Yes, you received a blow, but it's not only that. You feel a hangover, but you didn't have anything to drink, right? These are the first symptoms. Our clients, so to speak, don't notice that side effect because, let's not pretend, they are often heavy drinkers. Perfect, no?" Ulf didn't feel like answering. "Don't worry, you will die naturally, at least for an outside observer. I don't know when it will happen: to-day, in a month. People react differently." He laughed. "This new serum of ours is perfect. It removes evidence as well. You can go now."

Ulf got up with an effort and got closer to the desk. Smith allowed him to get near and nodded to his security guard approvingly. Ulf sat at the chair, and

Smith was sitting in his armchair with his legs on his desk.

"You know, Smith, a scumbag, or whatever is your name, if I'm going to die anyway, then tell me, what is this all for?"

"What for? Don't be stupid. Ah, one thing we have al-ready established," he said mockingly. "Power and money—in a way, they're both the same. What do you think, who backs me up? Money and power—this one percentage of the population who decide about everything in this world. And we need to make sure it stays this way. I mean: they take care of it, I'm focusing on business. They care about passing on their genes, without any strangers in the bloodline. They want a complete domination for themselves and for the next generations. I try not to involve myself in this, I only make money and give them a guarantee that everything stays within a family. They get their immortality. They like this word…

He paused and continued almost nostalgically. "Ulf, you were definitely good in what you did for us. Thanks to you, a lot of important children are going to be born, and I made a ton of money. But you"—he sighed—"you will not have anything left soon. Think about it, these are not your children." He leaned over closer toward Ulf, and added with a smile. "But don't worry. I will replace you easily."

He didn't know why, but he was filled with anger.

He flexed his muscles. Ulf knew that if he pushed hard with his legs and jumped, he could get him. "You, scumbag!" He pushed his legs against the floor and bounced toward Smith. Before he managed to leave the floor, the massive hand of the security guard pressed him back toward the chair. The fingers hurt his skin and almost broke his collar bone. He hissed with pain and looked at the big guy, who smiled with satisfaction.

"Are you trying to say you have some method to genetically modify the sperm?" Ulf asked.

"Amazing, right? I don't know much about it, but our eggheads tried to explain it to me. They said it's actually quite simple. You just need some genetic modification, and the body starts to produce sperm with a specific genotype."

"Why can't you do it in a more traditional way, like in vitro?"

"In vitro is outdated. We have had many unsuccessful attempts. This method is more efficient. There is also one more reason. I'm not sure if I should tell you, but since you are going to die anyway…Not everyone agrees to the experiment, so sometimes we steal the genetic material. We will take over and create our own elite. I see in your eyes that you cannot follow. Never mind. And women? Do you remember they looked at you when you met them? Thy also desired sex, especially with people whose sperm you carried."

"What do you mean?"

"It's an excellent setup for women, of course, if they are rich. Thanks to us they can have an ideal child and a protection of a male who cares for his offspring's well-being. A perfect investment: they give birth to a child, and in return, they have money and care. Yes, they didn't want you—they wanted the person whose sperm you are carrying, so theoretically, they didn't have sex with you, but with some other guy. And they would pay me for that. Perfect!"

"OK, if they want it, and your customers want their offspring, why don't they fertilize the women themselves?"

"Well, somehow, you're right. I hear only arguments that they want to stay hidden, they're looking after their reputation, or they have no time. Ridiculous, isn't it? As if they wanted to have children but do not necessarily want to meet their mothers. Excuses, but I do not ask.

I only agree with fake understanding and count the money." He grinned roughly. "I think they are merely corporate impotents. They are so busy multiplying money and maintaining power that it consumes all their energy. They are not even capable of fertilizing and they are ashamed of that, but that's just my opinion. Therefore, we need people like you, Ulf."

He got up from behind the desk and stood to face a

window, looking into the distance.

"You know what the funniest thing about all of this is? He continued his monolog. "It's so simple to find you, convince you under the premise of change or therapy or often sex. I guess it must be the fault of the media. Higher purpose!" He laughed out loud. "You are like a bunny who wants to spread your sperm around as much as possible. Human nature cannot be changed. Eh, don't worry. We won't kill you. You're dead already. And useless. You don't have a position or status for people to believe you. You can go now." He looked at his security guard, who obediently put his hand on Ulf's shoulder.

"And Frank? Have you seen him on TV, the police are on it," Ulf said impulsively.

"An overdose. Police don't have a clue, and the rest doesn't care. Anyway, why am I still talking to you? You are already dead." He nodded again at his body-guard. "Throw him out on the street."

The security guard silently grabbed his hand, strongly twisted it, and led him out of the building onto the road.

Ulf had nowhere to go, so he headed home. He didn't think about his coming death—he was quietly furious. He regretted not injecting the serum when he was in the lab. He would probably get some disease or infection, but at least he would prolong his life. He was planning his revenge on the way home. He felt as if his sexual energy converted into energy to avenge what had happened to him. He wanted to go back and kill Smith or wait on the street and get him when he leaves the building, but he was too tired. He wanted to lie down and fall asleep. He really did feel useless. He shambled all the way to his apartment. As he was lying in bed, he wanted to get rid of all his sperm, although he knew that would be impossible. He masturbated until his testicles stopped working. It lasted about an hour. At some point, he noticed that his hands were bloody and there was a wound on his penis. He didn't have any strength left to patch it up. Then he fell asleep. He was dreaming of all the women he had slept with. It was probably the first time he saw them clearly and in detail. He never remembered the way they looked, only some part, like the eyes, for example. Now he saw them clearly: facial lines, the color of their hair and eyes, their posture, the shape of their breasts. All of the women appeared in a big, round hall with no windows. It was painted white. It turned out to be a hospital ward but with no beds. That is when he noticed all of them were pregnant. They felt pain and started to give birth simultaneously. They lay with their vaginas directed toward him. He saw the infants' heads coming out of their dilated vaginas. The women would give birth on their own, and after they had finished, they were hugging their babies. When the infants turned their heads, the sight of them struck him. He flinched and backed off toward the wall. He was terrified. The babies had adult faces of grown women and men. Some of them he even recognized, like the loathed face of Smith. He wanted to run away, but there were no doors, so he started to kick against the wall. Meanwhile, the women let go of their children, and all the babies started crawling toward him with knives. He realized he would be murdered. He gave up and sat on the floor waiting for the unavoidable. As they were getting closer, he recognized that it's only a dream so they couldn't hurt him, but he also understood he would not wake up. It was the drug. Now he would die in his sleep. He was angry. He couldn't believe this is the end. And the worst of all was the feeling that it's not his time yet. He still had things to do. He felt incomplete and aware that he left nothing in the world. He desired to continue dreaming, even if those bastards would be chopping him apart—to dream as long as he could, so death wouldn't come during such a terrible nightmare.

He stopped dreaming and didn't wake up.

He was found naked in bed. His hands and penis were bloody. Some doctor leaned over, touching his body. Next to him, two paramedics waited with a stretcher, laughing under their breath. The doctor stated some-thing, and the description of this case became a popular anecdote among the medical staff.

An Animalish Man: How often do guys think about sex

www.ingramcontent.com/pod-product-compliance
Lightning Source LLC
Chambersburg PA
CBHW030513130626
46549CB00007B/2979